6/98

Raven
and River

For the Jeffers: Nancy, Denny, Jamie, and Kimmi — great friends in the Great Land! With love — N. W. C.

Rave on, skookum bird! — J. V. Z.

Text copyright © 1997 by Nancy White Carlstrom
Illustrations copyright © 1997 by Jon Van Zyle

First Edition

Library of Congress Cataloging-in-Publication Data

Carlstrom, Nancy White.
　　Raven and river / by Nancy White Carlstrom ; illustrated by Jon Van Zyle. — 1st ed.
　　p. cm.
　　ISBN 0-316-12894-5
　　[1. Raven and the other animals try to awaken the frozen river to the coming Alaskan springtime. 2. Ravens — Fiction. 3. Rivers — Fiction. 4. Alaska — Fiction. 5. Spring — Fiction. 6. Animals — Fiction.] I. Van Zyle, Jon, ill. II. Title.
PZ7.C21684Rav 1997
[Fic] — dc20　　　　　　　　　　　　　　　　　　　　　　　　95-14773

10 9 8 7 6 5 4 3 2 1

IM

Published simultaneously in Canada by
Little, Brown & Company (Canada) Limited

Printed in Singapore

The paintings in this book
were done in acrylics
on untempered
Masonite panels.
The text was
set in Tiepolo Bold
by AR Editions.

Raven
and River

by
Nancy White Carlstrom

Illustrated by Jon Van Zyle

 Little, Brown and Company
Boston New York Toronto London

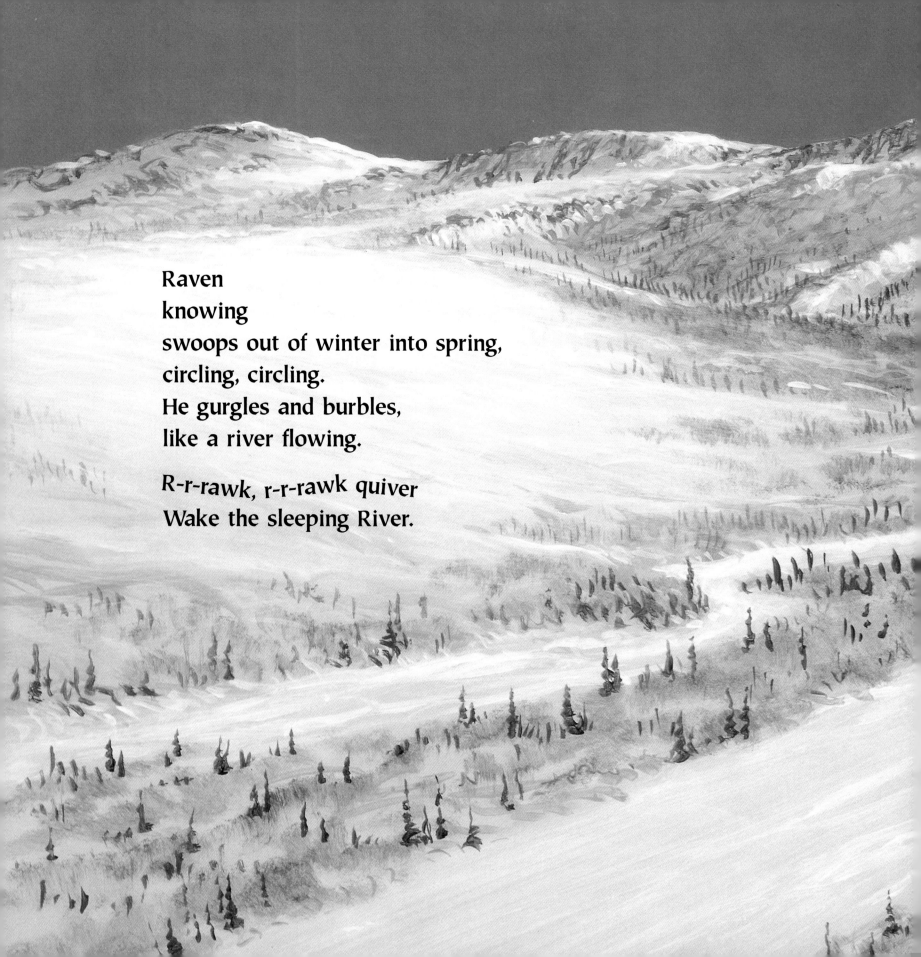

Raven
knowing
swoops out of winter into spring,
circling, circling.
He gurgles and burbles,
like a river flowing.

R-r-rawk, r-r-rawk quiver
Wake the sleeping River.

Red squirrel
listening
skitters up the highest spruce.
She searches this way, that way, back again.
Bright eyes sparkle,
like a river shining.

Chit-chit shimmer
Wake the sleeping River.

Ruffed grouse
strutting
rearranges feathers.
He beats his wings,
like a river humming.

Thum-thum thither
Wake the sleeping River.

Wolf
rising
climbs out of her own sleep
up the steep cliff.
She raises her head and howls, then takes off,
like a river running.

Yowl-yowl *shiver*
Wake the sleeping River.

Snowshoe hare
twitching
leaps to the air.
In two-color coat,
she bounds over familiar paths,
like a river dancing.

Run-run *hither*
Wake the sleeping River.

Bear
yawning
gets up from dreams of fish.
Big-pawed and groggy,
he enters the light,
like a river turning.

Slap-flap dither
Wake the sleeping River.

Beaver
waiting
is not surprised.
For in his old winter lodge
he feels the ice begin to shift,
like a river moving.

Crick-crack *sliver*
The River The River.

Raven circles and circles and circles.

R-r-rawk, r-r-rawk quiver
Chit-chit shimmer
Thum-thum thither
Yowl-yowl shiver
Run-run hither
Slap-flap dither
Crick-crack sliver
Circle for the Giver
The River The River

River squints through eyes of ice.
She stretches and stretches and stretches,
waking up
breaking up.

R-r-rawk, r-r-rawk quiver

Then River
shimmers for red squirrel,
hums with ruffed grouse,
runs after wolf,
and dances with snowshoe hare.

River turns over with fish for bear
and moves in a new home for beaver.

And Raven—
Raven dips and soars
dips and soars
cutting the bright blue cloth of a sky
tumbling
flying
swooping
crying.

Together
Raven and River
gurgle and burble and roll their *r*'s

R-r-rawk, r-r-rawk quiver
Circle for the Giver
Rr-rip-rip Raven Rr-rip-rip River
Rippling rippling rippling

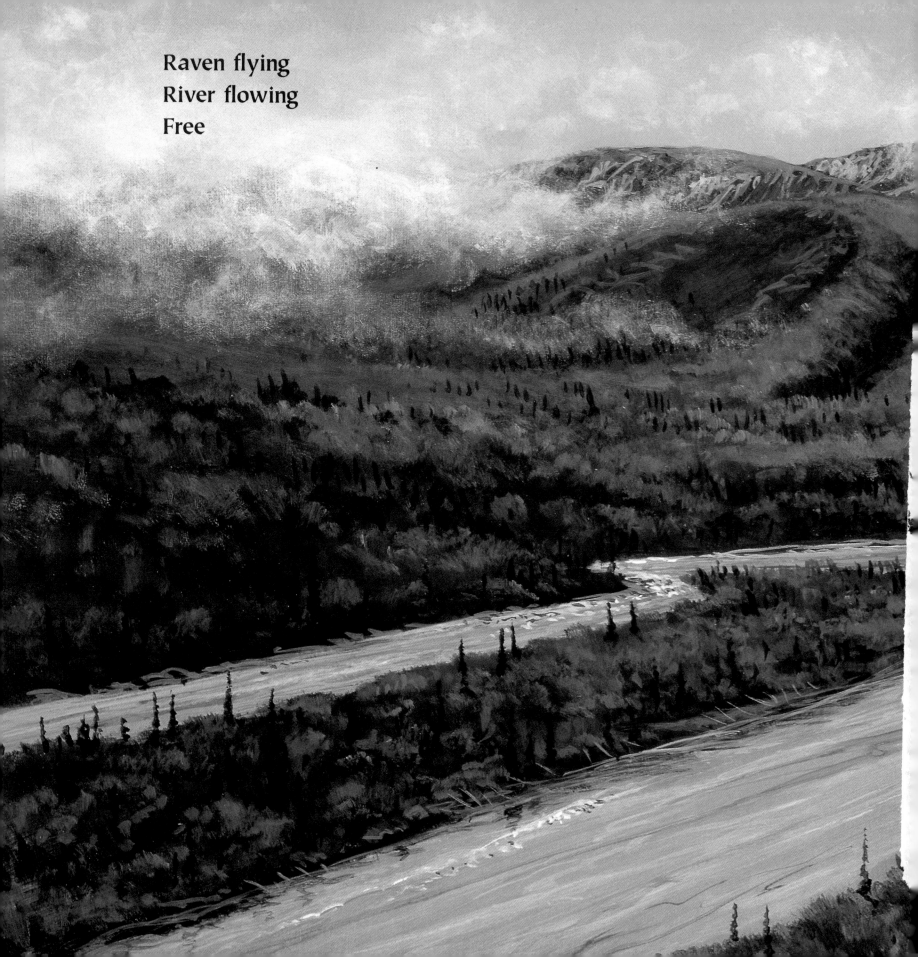

Raven flying
River flowing
Free

Author's Note

Raven and River are part of our daily lives here in Fairbanks, Alaska, where I live. The Raven, so black against the white Alaskan landscape in winter, is much more than a scavenger. I have seen him tumble through a blue sky, soar fluidly over the treetops, and land at my feet, cocking his head as if to say, "Of course, I know it's forty below zero. So what?"

Likewise, the River is a strong presence. In the winter, it freezes and becomes a highway to snow machines, skis, and dogsleds. In one place, called the "ice bridge," even cars and trucks cross over the thick ice.

By the first week of May, one can usually see huge ice chunks crashing dramatically downstream. Spring is one short month of melting snow, oozing mud, and budding leaves.

During this, the time of breakup, it is common to hear the Raven's throaty gurgle, sounding like running water, as it flies over the changing landscape. The Raven's call always reminds me of the waking River.

— N. W. C.